WHO'S HIDING?

Guess! Then lift
the flaps to find out!

By Naomi Kleinberg

A Random House PICTUREBACK® Book

Random House 🏠 New York

"Sesame Workshop,"® "Sesame Street,"® and associated characters, trademarks, and design elements are owned and licensed by Sesame Workshop. Copyright © 2017 by Sesame Workshop. All Rights Reserved. Published in the United States by Random House Children's Books, a division of Penguin Random House LLC, 1745 Broadway, New York, NY 10019, and in Canada by Penguin Random House Canada Limited, Toronto, in conjunction with Sesame Workshop. Pictureback, Random House, and the Random House colophon are registered trademarks of Penguin Random House LLC.
randomhousekids.com
SesameStreetBooks.com
www.sesamestreet.org
Educators and librarians, for a variety of teaching tools, visit us at RHTeachersLibrarians.com
ISBN 978-1-5247-1634-9
MANUFACTURED IN CHINA
10 9 8 7 6 5 4 3 2
Random House Children's Books supports the First Amendment and celebrates the right to read.

ANIMAL CYCLE

NATURE'S CYCLES

Ray James

Rourke
Publishing LLC
Vero Beach, Florida 32964

www.rourkepublishing.com

PHOTO CREDITS: All Photographs © Lynn M. Stone

Editor: Robert Stengard-Olliges

Cover and interior design by Nicola Stratford

Library of Congress Cataloging-in-Publication Data

Stone, Lynn M.
 Animal cycle / Lynn M. Stone.
   p. cm. -- (Nature's cycle)
 ISBN 1-60044-175-0
 1. Animal life cycles--Juvenile literature. I. Title. II. Series: Stone, Lynn M. Nature's cycle.
 QL49.S785 2007
 591.56--dc22   2006013442

Printed in the USA

CG/CG

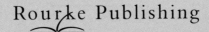

Rourke Publishing

www.rourkepublishing.com – sales@rourkepublishing.com
Post Office Box 3328, Vero Beach, FL 32964

Table of Contents

Animal Life Cycles

The life of each animal travels from birth to death. We call that **journey** the animal's life cycle.

Animals are all different. They belong to many different groups.

The life cycles of animals are somewhat different.
They are somewhat alike, too.

Animal Reproduction

The story of any animal begins with a spark of life.
That comes about through **reproduction**.

Male and female animals **mate**. By mating, they reproduce more of their own kind. Without reproduction, animals would disappear.

Animal Birth

A baby animal grows within its mother or within an egg. One day the baby is born.

After it is born, an animal grows. It grows by eating proper food. Its body changes.

Animal Growth

Some animals go through separate **stages** of life. Insects, for example, may have two or three stages of life after birth.

During these stages, many young insects may look nothing like their parents.

Many other animals, though, look like small adults even at birth!

Each animal that grows up will one day look very much like one of its parents. Then it will be an adult.

Adult animals reproduce. Their babies begin new life cycles.

Animal Death

Animal lives may be short or long. Some animals live only for hours or days.

Others can live for more than 100 years.

All animals die. They can die from many causes.
Some are eaten by other animals.

Sooner or later, their remains become part of soil and water. In that way, dead animals become food and **vitamins** for living animals.

Glossary

journey (JUR nee) — a long trip

mate (MATE) — to join together for breeding

reproduction (ree pruh DUNHK shuhn) — the making of more of the same plant or animal

stages (STAY jez) — the major periods in an animals life

vitamin (VE tuh min) — a substance in food needed for good health

INDEX

FURTHER READING

Ehlert, Lois. *Waiting for Wings*. Harcourt, 2001.
Ganeri, Anita. *Animal Life Cycles*. Heinemann, 2005.

WEBSITES TO VISIT

http://esd.iu5.org/LessonPlans/LifeCycle/animals.htm

ABOUT THE AUTHOR :

Ray James writes children's fiction and nonfiction. A former teacher, Ray understands what kids like to read. Ray lives with his wife and three cats in Gary, Indiana.